For Eleanor–R. B.

SIMON & SCHUSTER BOOKS FOR YOUNG READERS · An imprint of Simon & Schuster Children's Publishing Division · 1230 Avenue of the Americas, New York, New York 10020 · Text copyright © 2020 by Robert Broder · Illustrations copyright © 2020 by Olivier Tallec · All rights reserved, including the right of reproduction in whole or in part in any form. · SIMON & SCHUSTER BOOKS FOR YOUNG READERS is a trademark of Simon & Schuster, Inc. · For information about special discounts for bulk purchases, please contact Simon & Schuster Special Sales at 1-866-506-1949 or business@simonandschuster.com. · The Simon & Schuster Speakers Bureau can bring authors to your live event. For more information or to book an event, contact the Simon & Schuster Speakers Bureau at 1-866-248-3049 or visit our website at www.simonspeakers.com. · Book design by Lucy Ruth Cummins · The text for this book was set in Baskerville. · The illustrations for this book were rendered in acrylic and pencils on paper. · Manufactured in China · 0820 SCP · First Edition · 10 9 8 7 6 5 4 3 2 1 · Library of Congress Cataloging-in-Publication Data · Names: Broder, Robert, author. | Tallec, Olivier, illustrator. · Title: Crow and Snow / Robert Broder ; illustrated by Olivier Tallec.· Description: First edition. | New York : Simon & Schuster Books for Young Readers, [2020] | Summary: · Crow, a scarecrow, is lonely standing in the cornfield until the farmer's children build a snowman next to him, starting a years-long friendship. · Identifiers: LCCN 2019013290 | ISBN 9781534445956 (hardcover) | ISBN 9781534445963 (eBook) · Subjects: | CYAC: Scarecrows—Fiction. | Snowmen—Fiction. | Friendship—Fiction. · Classification: LCC PZ7.1.B75756 Cro 2020 | DDC [E]—dc23 · LC record available at https://lccn.loc.gov/2019013290

Crow & Snow

robert broder &
olivier tallec

Simon & Schuster
Books for Young Readers
New York   London
Toronto   Sydney   New Delhi

One spring a farmer built a scarecrow.

Crow tried to say hello to the tractor as it passed.

"Hello!"
said Crow.

"Hello?"
said Crow.

But the tractor never said hello back.

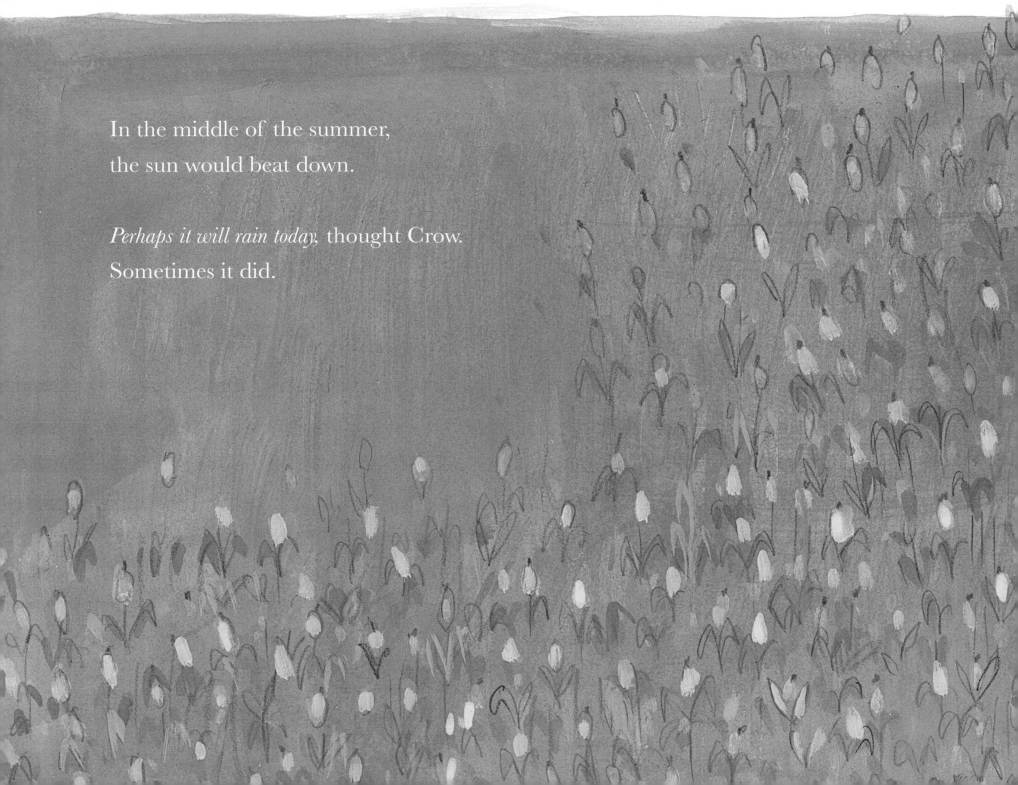

In the middle of the summer,
the sun would beat down.

Perhaps it will rain today, thought Crow.
Sometimes it did.

Winter came.

The corn was gone, and Crow didn't see much of the farmer.

It was windy and gray.

Crow just stood there.

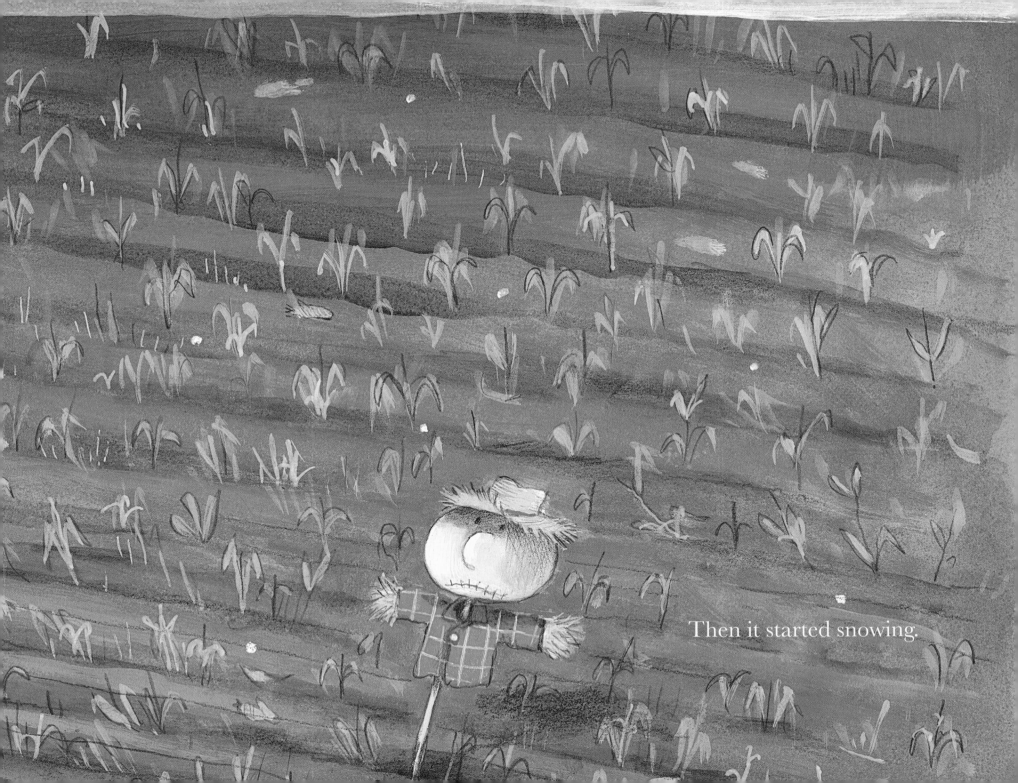

Then it started snowing.

The farmer's children ran outside and rolled and rolled the snow into an enormous ball.

They rolled another ball until . . .

they had built a snowman right next to Crow.

Crow and the snowman stood side by side.

Crow wondered if he should say something.

"Hello," said Crow.
"Hello," said Snow.

"It's nice to have someone out
in this field with me," said Crow.
"It certainly is a nice field," said Snow.

Crow tried to think of something else to say.

"I like your scarf," said Crow.

"Thank you," said Snow. "I like your hat."

"Will you be staying awhile?" asked Crow.

"I'm not sure," said Snow. "Maybe."

And Crow and Snow stood side by side.

The days became warmer.

"Are you leaving?" asked Crow.

"It seems that way," said Snow.

"Will you come back?" asked Crow.

"I'm not sure," said Snow. "Maybe."

"Well, I certainly have enjoyed your company," said Crow.
But Snow was already gone.

All through the spring Crow stood tall and alone in the field.
The farmer plowed, planted, and watered.

The tractor drove by without saying hello.
Crow couldn't help thinking about Snow.

Another harvest went by,

and it started snowing.

"Why hello," said Crow. "Nice to see you again."

"Yes, indeed," said Snow. "Nice to see you again."

"You look a bit different," said Crow.

"You look about the same," said Snow.

And the two friends stood side by side.

One bitterly cold day, a blizzard covered
Crow and Snow in a blanket of white.

"I like it under here," said Crow.
"Me too," said Snow. "It's like our own little home."

Crow was happy.

Until . . .

the days
became warmer.

"Snow," said Crow.
"Yes?" said Snow.

"I will miss you," said Crow.
"I will miss you too," said Snow.

And he was gone.

As the seasons passed, the tractor and the corn came and went, and the children grew older.

And every winter Snow would return and stand next to Crow.

One winter it snowed so
much, the children built a
second snowman.
"Who is that? asked Crow.
"I'm not sure," said Snow.
"It sure does feel crowded
out here," said Crow.
"It certainly does,"
agreed Snow.

The visitor did not stay long.

And as the sun rose higher in the sky, neither did Snow.

When Snow returns, thought Crow, *I will tell him how I feel.*

But many years passed where
the children didn't come out to play,
so Crow never saw Snow.

Then one winter, new children came and rolled and
rolled the snow into an enormous ball.

"Welcome back!" said Crow, excitedly.

"It's good to be back," said Snow. "I see you have a new hat."

"Yes," said Crow. "The last one blew away."

"Well, I like it," said Snow.

Crow wondered if he could say what he was feeling.

One night a strong wind came bursting across the field and knocked Crow over.

"You caught me,"
said Crow.
"It's the least
I can do,"
said Snow.

It was quiet.
"Snow," said Crow.
"Yes," said Snow.

"I love you," said Crow.

"I love you too," said Snow.

Crow and Snow stood side by side. They were happy.